The Seal

by Liza Charlesworth

ISBN: 978-1-338-84448-1

Art Director: Tannaz Fassihi; Designer: Cynthia Ng; Illustrated by Michael Robertson
Copyright © Liza Charlesworth. All rights reserved. Published by Scholastic Inc.

2 3 4 5 68 26 25 24

Printed in Jiaxing, China. First printing, June 2022.

■SCHOLASTIC

Meet Seal.
Meet Eel.
The pals' home is
deep in the sea.

"It is time to race to the reef,"
Seal says to Eel.
"1, 2, 3, go!" says Whale.

3

Race, race, race!
Seal is fast.
Eel is not.

4

Seal is in the lead.
So Seal says,
"I can take a seat."

5

Seal has time to eat
a huge meal.

Seal has time
to make
a cute mule.

Seal has time to read a fine tale
set in the deep sea.

Seal has time to take
a nice nap.
Zzzzzzzzzzzzzzzzzzz!

Eel is not fast.
But Eel will not stop.
Race, race, race!

Poke, poke, poke!
"Wake up, Seal," says Whale.
"Eel is in the lead."

Race, race, race!
Seal is near the reef.
Can Seal beat Eel?

NOPE!
The race is close.
But Eel wins it by a nose.

"I hate to fail," said Seal.
"But I am not sad.
Eel is a nice, nice pal!"

13

Read & Review

Invite your learner to point to each long-vowel word and read it aloud.

i_e
nice
fine
time

o_e
nope
home
nose
poke
close

a_e
race
make
hate
tale
take
wake
whale

ea

seal

read

beat

lead

near

sea

meal

ee

deep

eat

seat

reef

u_e

eel

huge

meet

ai

cute

mule

fail

15

Fun Fill-Ins

Read the sentences aloud, inviting your learner to complete them using the long-vowel words in the box.

> Eel   tale   time   nose   mule

1. The race is between Seal and

   _____.

2. Seal takes a seat because she thinks she has a lot of _____.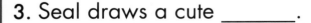

3. Seal draws a cute _____.

4. Seal reads a fine _____.

5. At the end, Eel wins by a _____.